P9-DZN-553

Hana Hashimoto,
SIXTH VIOLIN

To my friends and family, for their cherished support and encouragement; for Paul, as ever, and for Aiko, especially — C.U.

To Flora, for sharing her love of music — Q. L.

Kids Can Press acknowledges the financial support of the Government of Ontario, through the Ontario Media Development Corporation's Ontario Book Initiative; the Ontario Arts Council; the Canada Council for the Arts; and the Government of Canada, through the CBF, for our publishing activity.

Published in Canada by
Kids Can Press Ltd.
25 Dockside Drive
Toronto, ON M5A 0B5

Published in the U.S. by
Kids Can Press Ltd.
2250 Military Road
Tonawanda, NY 14150

www.kidscanpress.com

The artwork in this book was rendered in pencil and colored digitally.
The text is set in Brosio Pro.

Edited by Yasemin Uçar
Designed by Karen Powers

This book is smyth sewn casebound.
Manufactured in Shenzhen, China, in 02/2014 by C & C Offset

CM 14 0 9 8 7 6 5 4 3 2 1

Library and Archives Canada Cataloguing in Publication

Uegaki, Chieri, author
Hana Hashimoto, sixth violin / written by Chieri Uegaki ; illustrated by Qin Leng.

ISBN 978-1-894786-33-1 (bound)

I. Leng, Qin, illustrator II. Title.

PS8591.E32H35 2014 jC813'.6 C2013-908216-6

Kids Can Press is a Corus™ Entertainment company

Hana Hashimoto, SIXTH VIOLIN

WRITTEN BY CHIERI UEGAKI ILLUSTRATED BY QIN LENG

KIDS CAN PRESS

When Hana Hashimoto announced that she had signed up for the talent show and that she would be playing the violin, her brothers nearly fell out of a tree.

"That's just loopy," said Kenji. "You're still a beginner."

"Stop kidding," said Koji. "You can barely play a note."

"It's a *talent* show, Hana."

"You'll be a disaster!"

Hana squared her shoulders and took her violin and bow inside, leaving her brothers laughing like monkeys in the tree.

She pulled at the strings, letting them twang. It was true that she was still a beginner. She had only been to three lessons.

The first time Hana held a real violin had been that summer, while visiting her grandfather in Japan.

Long, long ago, her grandfather had been part of a great symphony orchestra in Kyoto. Ojiichan had been Second Violin and once played in front of the Imperial Family.

Ojiichan played every morning. From his study, the clear, bright notes would drift upstairs, through the shoji screen doors to where Hana slept on sweet-smelling tatami mats, and coax her awake as gently as sunshine.

Ojiichan usually played classical pieces by Mozart or Mendelssohn or Bach. But in the indigo evenings, while Hana and her brothers ate ice cream and oranges, Ojiichan would sit on the veranda and play requests.

Hana always asked for a song about a crow cawing for her seven chicks. Whenever Ojiichan played it, Hana would feel a shiver of happy-sadness ripple through her.

Ojiichan didn't just play songs. He could also make his violin chirp like the crickets Hana tried to find in the tall grasses.

He could pluck the strings to mimic the sound of raindrops on the oil-paper umbrella Hana twirled under during summer storms.

And when the first fireflies emerged at twilight, Ojiichan could compose a melody that seemed to make them dance higher and glow brighter than ever before.

At the end of each day, as Hana lay with her head resting on a cool buckwheat pillow, Ojiichan would play a lullaby so soothing that sleep would fall over her like a blanket.

On their last day together, Hana told Ojiichan that she wanted to learn to play the violin. And when Hana got home, her parents agreed that she could.

Now, Hana was practicing not just for lessons, but for the talent show, too.

Hana practiced every day, just like Ojiichan. And every day, her brothers fled the house with covered ears, complaining about the horrible noise.

She practiced in front of her parents, who listened with care while they washed and dried the dishes.

She practiced in front of her dog, Jojo, who cocked his head and sometimes growled at the strange sounds Hana made.

And she practiced on her own, in front of an old photo of Ojiichan from his symphony days. Alone, Hana could pretend she was performing in front of an audience so appreciative they called for encore after encore.

The day of the talent show arrived and the school auditorium thrummed with excitement. Backstage, Hana waited with a walloping heart. A dozen acts, including five other violinists, had already gone before her.

Finally, Hana heard the master of ceremonies call her name.

As Hana walked onto the stage, her violin tucked under her arm and bow gripped tight in her hand, an oceanic roar filled her ears.

Things seemed to be moving in slow motion, and for one dizzy moment, Hana thought, "Kenji and Koji were right. This is going to be a disaster." She wished she could turn into a grain of rice and disappear into a crack between the floorboards.

She could hardly see with the spotlight in her eyes. Yet, as Hana looked out into the audience, certain faces appeared to her, as if through a telescopic lens.

She could see her brothers, melting into their seats.

She saw her best friend, Jas, giving her two thumbs up.

And there, her smiling mother, and her father, camera in hand.

Hana held a breath, then ballooned her cheeks before letting it out. With a *whoosh,* the roaring in her ears receded. Then, as everyone seemed to disappear beyond the light shining down on her like a moonbeam, she remembered.

"Gambarunoyo, Hana-chan." Do your best, her grandfather had told her. Ojiichan would be cheering for her.

Hana swallowed her nerves like medicine and leaned toward the microphone. She would just do her best.

"This is the sound of a mother crow calling her chicks," she said. She placed the violin under her chin, held her bow in position and played three raw, squawky notes.

"This is the sound of my neighbor's cat at night." She dragged the bow across the strings and the violin yowled in loud protest.

"This is the sound of rain on a paper umbrella." Hana plucked the strings for a soothing *plomp-plomp-plomp*.

As Hana continued to play all the special sounds she had practiced, the air around her came alive with buzzing bees ...

... and lowing cows

... and squeaking mice

... and croaking frogs.

Finally, as the last sound effect trailed away, Hana tucked her bow and violin under her arm. "And that," she said to the audience, "is how I play the violin."

Then she took a great big bow.

Later, after dinner, Kenji surprised Hana by asking for an encore. “Make that funny cow sound again,” he said.

Then Koji said, “Make that crazy cat sound, too.”

So Hana did. And when her mother and father and brothers all laughed, she happily played her sounds again.

Perhaps next year Hana would be able to perform one of Ojiichan's favorite pieces. But for now, Hana played a little melody she had been practicing, remembered from nights lit by dancing fireflies. She imagined that the notes would drift out through the window, past the bright rabbit moon and beyond, and Ojiichan would hear them and smile.